FR. 33108

*For Esi*

*Angel Boy* copyright © Frances Lincoln Limited 2008
Text copyright © Bernard Ashley 2008

First published in Great Britain in 2008 and in the USA in 2009 by
Frances Lincoln Children's Books, 4 Torriano Mews,
Torriano Avenue, London NW5 2RZ
www.franceslincoln.com

First paperback edition 2009

British Library Cataloguing in Publication Data
available on request

ISBN 978-1-84507-809-6

Set in Baskerville

1 3 5 7 9 8 6 4 2

Printed in the United Kingdom

# Bernard Ashley

**F**

FRANCES LINCOLN
CHILDREN'S BOOKS

# Chapter One

**H**e was definitely going to do it. Only a week of the school holiday gone and the rest of it stretching into the distance like an empty sea that would take forever to cross. Thirty-five days to go, eight hundred and forty hours: and how sad was it to be longing for the start of term?

Life was on heavy time for Leonard Boameh. Nana was no fun, sweeping his feet off with her broom, elbowing him away from her hot pots, reaching her long fingers at him for yesterday's shirt off his back, too busy for a tickle these days – all the while singing the same old hymns in her high church voice: *What a friend we have in Jesus….!* Well, a friend like Jesus could do Leonard a favour right now – by turning up for a game of something. Any friend would have been fun, but Leonard's house was too far from Blessed Wisdom Primary for him to invite his school mates, and the Cantonment District Elementary School kids who lived nearby didn't want to know him.

So he was going to do it. He'd made up his mind.

His dad was great. When his dad was home they kicked a ball around outside, and argued about Manchester United and Accra Hearts of Oak in the Ghana Premiership, and looked over each other's shoulders at the news from the *Graphic Sports*. They jaunted out in the car and brought back pizza and McDonalds, they squeezed together in an armchair and watched the English football beamed up from South Africa, and they had sessions on the internet. But his dad wasn't home that much, and Nana was no substitute. Even if Leonard could get her outside, she couldn't head a ball, she never dived for a low shot when she was in goal, and the internet made her flap her hands at the computer and go rattling on about the superiority of books.

So he had to do it, he just had to.

He'd tried to get himself out of the place another way, but he couldn't. He'd had a go at persuading his dad to let him go to work with him. But his dad worked out of the Nile Hotel and didn't want him around. No, he would have liked him around, he said, but it wasn't appropriate.

What *was* appropriate was for his dad to polish his car and clean the cracked windscreen and vacuum the red dust off the floor mats – and then most days he'd be doing a job for one of the hotel clients. He'd take them into town, to Makola Market, or to the National Cultural Centre, or the Nkruma Museum; or, with his overnight holdall in the boot, he'd take them off on a trip. Without warning to Nana, except for a message from his mobile, he'd go up-country to the Mole National Park, or to the weaving sheds where Kente cloth was made, or along the coast to the slave forts. But even if there was a spare seat in the car, Leonard couldn't sit in it – the clients wouldn't want it, his dad said.

And his dad would be away for days. Leonard would get his nightly phone call, and be told to be good for Nana, night-night, God bless. But Leonard didn't think Nana was good for *him*. She was getting to be a really old person.

So he was definitely going to make his break, just for a few hours. And today was the day.

When he'd washed to Nana's satisfaction, he put on his second-best school shirt, the redness slightly faded by the pummel of Nana's tub. It was a careful choice, because he could wear it with his shorts and still look serious, with the holy cross on the pocket badge giving off a look of piety. At school all the boys had to wear shorts, and Leonard's dad insisted that he wear them in the holidays, too. 'Relish your childhood!' he'd say.

'Kids grow up too fast!' Of course, Nana went along with that, and Leonard had no mother to appeal to – she had died when he was born.

He emptied his wooden pot of the ten thousand-*cedie* notes he'd saved, and tucked them in his pocket. He put a bottle of water and some fruit into his school slipper-bag and pulled the drawstring tight. It was ten o'clock and at this hour the minibuses everyone called *tro-tros* wouldn't be too full of people going to work. And, not wanting to tell any lies to Nana, he drifted out to the yard as if he was going to play a game – and slipped out through the gate at the side.

Leonard Boameh was away on his own day trip.

❀ ❀ ❀

He walked through the back alleys to Nsawam Road, the best place in Accra to find a tro-tro. They stopped wherever you stood waving at them, with a driver's mate hanging out shouting for business and taking the money. Everyone shifted up along the seats to let new people in, mostly going into the town – but tro-tros went up-country and east and west, too – it all depended which roadside you stood on. They were cheaper than state-run buses, and the railways were hopeless.

But Leonard had got it wrong. Crowds of people were standing waiting for tro-tros on Nsawam Road. It was a busy day for Makola Market. Women and boys were still walking there, bowls balanced on their heads with fruit and iced water and stacked-up toilet rolls. The sight of the iced water reminded Leonard how hot and sweaty he felt, and wearing shorts suddenly didn't seem a bad idea at all.

Head held high, balancing his secret, he walked with the people going to market as far as the Cathedral roundabout and turned right on to Castle Road – where, although the tro-tros were fewer and further between, there were fewer people, too. And he didn't mind where he went, so long as it was away from Cantonment District for a few hours.

'You want towards Cape Coast, Elmina?' a tro-tro mate shouted at him, as a dusty minibus swerved into the kerb.

'How long does it take?' Leonard asked.

The mate cracked his fingers as if his arm was a whip. 'All the way – two hours, about.'

'How much?'

'Tell you when we get there. Come on, *abarima*!' He held the door open, and people moved along. The tro-tro was half-full, with a white backpacking couple as well as local people. Leonard knew that the more people there were in the bus, the cheaper the fare: but time was important, too. He had to get back by tea-time. He was sure he could afford about four hours away, though – so he got in.

As he settled on the hot seat, he planned his day. He'd be there and back well before the telephone call from his dad that evening. His dad was up-country until Friday, and although Leonard knew Nana would scold him, he wouldn't have to see his dad's disappointed look down the phone. And wouldn't his teacher approve of him going to Elmina?

Elmina was one of the places where the Europeans had built their forts for imprisoning slaves before they were shipped off in shackles to be sold in America. Children studied it in school, and if Leonard could say that he had seen with his own eyes 'the Door of No Return', then he would definitely get house points for putting his holidays to good use. He could take a quick look at the place while the driver and the mate got their dinner, and come back in the same tro-tro.

So his adventure would be useful, as well as getting him out of Accra for the day.

❀ ❀ ❀

He settled into his seat and enjoyed the breeze

through the open window as the tro-tro picked up speed on the coast road heading west. The other Africans in the tro-tro sounded as if they were going to Elmina to see their families, but the backpackers next to Leonard had a guide book between them. They were holidaymakers, the same as him, so Leonard offered them water from the bottle in his bag.

And, having made friends with them, Leonard told them a made-up tale about going to Elmina for holiday homework – doing what he hadn't done to Nana, telling lies… But going off on an adventure called for a little bending of the truth, didn't it?

## Chapter Two

The backpackers' names were Chris and Vicky, and they were from England. They were younger than his dad, but a bit older than Leonard's teacher at Blessed Wisdom. They were serious people, but they smiled a lot and agreed with each other in quiet voices – unlike the noisy people in the seats behind.

'Are you going to see the fort at Elmina?' Chris asked Leonard.

'Yes, I'm going to see the fort at Elmina,' Leonard told him – saying it loudly enough for everyone else in the tro-tro to hear.

'You learn about it at school?'

Leonard nodded, his head dangerously near to coming off his shoulders.

'Then would you come round with us? Tell us what you think…?'

'I surely will,' Leonard said, sagely.

'It would be good to get your impressions…'

In about the time the tro-tro mate had said, the bus arrived in Elmina. It dropped the gossipy women off in the town, near a knot of mean-looking street kids, their stares at Leonard through the glass making him turn his head in the other direction. It went on up to the fort with the three remaining passengers, where Leonard counted out his fare. It used up just about half of what he had.

'What time, here?' he wanted to know from the mate, needing to be sure that he'd get back home in time.

'You go around,' the mate said to Leonard and the backpackers, flicking his fingers at the fort. 'We come back…' And he nodded his head in the general direction of the small car park, as time to go was when things happened, not what numbers the hands of a clock pointed to. He banged on the roof for the driver to be off before they got embroiled in the commotion running up the track – a crowd of older kids chasing up from the car park and immediately surrounding the two backpackers.

'What's your name, Boss?'

'What's yours, Missus?'

'Where you from?'

'You got an e-mail address?'

Vicky walked on. 'He's Chris and I'm Vicky, from London.'

'London! England! We love England!' the boys called after them as Leonard hurried with his new friends up the slope to the fort entrance. 'Give England our love!'

Leonard kept his shirt well tucked in. He'd looked at the boys. For school holiday kids they were far too neat in their clean shirts and jeans: they looked more like students on a Sunday outing. By contrast, beyond the fort, down by the beach, men and boys were stripped off and sweating, hacking at big tree trunks to make dug-out fishing canoes. On a nearby stretch of land set up with goal posts other youths were playing football, everyone hot and scruffy. No one around Elmina looked as neatly turned out as these boys at the fort entrance – quite different from the raggedy boys Leonard had seen in the town, those kids with mean, hungry-looking faces. That scruffy lot had seemed threatening, but these tidy ones were puzzling. What was their game? Suddenly Leonard suddenly didn't feel so comfortable far away from home, and he hurried to keep up with the backpackers going into the fort.

But how was he going to go inside? His pocket money didn't take account of entrance fees. He just about had enough for the tro-tro back home. What should he do? Could he skulk just inside the entrance until Chris and Vicky came out? He didn't fancy being alone with either set of the

Elmina kids.

'Will you be our guest?' Vicky suddenly asked him, turning from the pay box.

'Sure, do us the honour of coming round with us?' Chris said.

To which Leonard was happy to say 'thank you'.

❀ ❀ ❀

They were in the company of a guide – a young woman who took them all over the fort, and didn't spare the horrors of the place. First, she stopped them at a plaque on the wall, and in a quiet voice read aloud the words on it.

**IN EVERLASTING MEMORY OF**
**THE ANGUISH OF OUR ANCESTORS.**
**MAY THOSE WHO DIED REST IN PEACE.**
**MAY THOSE WHO RETURN FIND THEIR ROOTS.**
**MAY HUMANITY NEVER AGAIN PERPETRATE**
**SUCH INJUSTICE AGAINST HUMANITY.**
**WE, THE LIVING, VOW TO UPHOLD THIS.**

She then asked the three of them to join her in their own silent prayers, and after shutting his eyes – and a sudden feeling of the rightness of coming here, standing where he was and praying for his forebears who had been treated so cruelly – Leonard took his cue from the others, and followed the guide, who had walked discreetly on.

Leonard knew from his history lessons what had happened in this place – but that didn't stop a swirling anger from burning inside him as he saw for himself the scenes of those terrible things. He found himself in those same dark, arched dungeons where there was no light, no sanitation. His breath seemed to leave him as he pressed his hands against the unforgiving walls of the dungeon where the women had been kept, some of them taken out to be abused by the slave traders and thrown back again.

He went down more steep steps, the same steps where the men had been pushed, shackled at the ankles in spiteful chains. He stood beneath the sculptured skull above a dark doorway and his stomach rolled with fear as he looked into the condemned cell where they had thrown men and women who disobeyed and locked the heavy door, until they died of thirst and hunger.

Leonard ran his hands down the walls, felt the rusted shackle-rings. And tears came to his eyes as he counted back in time the way his teacher had done in the history lesson. He was overcome by the feeling that he could almost touch his great-great-great-great Nana, who could almost have been sold as a slave. He pictured the anguish on such a sweet face, and he felt helplessness and horror and anger.

Finally he stood at the Door of No Return, that terrible, gate-like aperture, a sort of long, barred window in the thick wall. Through here the slaves were taken out and down to the canoes on the beach: this was the door through which no one who left was ever to come back to their homeland. It would be generations, Leonard knew, before their descendants would see this dreadful place.

He stood looking at the bright light coming in through the door, so bright against the dark inside that it was hard to see his backpacker friends in the shadows. And he heard the sound of quiet crying, at first imagining it was the ghost of one of those slaves. But it was Chris, and the guide, too – who came to this door many times a day, and was still so upset at times that she couldn't keep back the tears.

*The beginning of wisdom is knowing who you are.*
*Draw near and listen.*

She quoted the Swahili proverb to Leonard, and put a hand on his shoulder. And she told quietly of those who had gone through this door: mothers, fathers, brothers, sisters and children – stripped, branded and separated from each other for all time. She unlocked the door for them, to let them see down the steps to the canoes below.

Vicky took a photograph, and apologised for

doing so. And they left, passing one of the churches within the fort where the slave traffickers had worshipped, thinking there was nothing un-Christian about doing what they did.

So affected was Leonard by what he'd seen that he no longer felt that he was in the real-life world of today: it was like leaving a cinema wearing some other, imaginary, skin.

As soon as they came out of the fort, Chris and Vicky were surrounded by the smart boys who had met them going in, but now they had conch shells in their hands, painted with the names of their new English friends, the names that they'd eased out of them.

Chris was being given one. It was painted with the words:

**TO OUR BRITISH BROTHER MR CHRIS.**
**FROM YOUR BROTHERS ISAAC,**
**TIM AND FREDERICK.**
**HAVE A NICE TRIP.**
**Isaacweston23@yahoo.com AT ELMINA CASTLE.**

And Vicky had the same, except that she was an honorary sister.

Suddenly Leonard realised what these boys were up to: now they were hounding the backpackers all the way down the slope, demanding American dollars for their conch shell gifts. It was what Leonard's father called 'a scam'.

❀ ❀ ❀

It was while the backpackers were busy finding dollars as they hurried back to the tro-tro, arguing and shaking their heads when whatever they offered was not enough, that their attention went off their young friend from Accra.

As the group moved on, Leonard was suddenly surrounded by three of the scruffy street kids from the town. They grabbed him, mean and menacing.

'You come with us!' their leader said – a kid with a tribal-cut face and a twisted mouth.

'We got you!'

And all at once Leonard was off his feet and being carried, squirming and shouting, down to the teeming town, unheard by anyone who mattered.

What sort of a terrible adventure was this?

# Chapter Three

The back ends of most poor towns are tips. People live in shacks, if they're lucky, or else they sleep wherever their hungry bodies fall down. The have-nots are left to scavenge in the town's rubbish amid the sickly smell of burning in empty oil drums, where fires blacken the food cans and beer tins that might be sold for scrap. Here, under rusted corrugated sheeting, was where the street kids lived – the place to which they frog-marched Leonard. The three who had captured him were joined by others as he was taken struggling over the harbour bridge and past the huts and fishing boats. No one paid this group of homeless kids much attention. Homeless kids and beggars were everywhere around towns like Elmina.

Desperately, Leonard tried to catch someone's eyes or ears. But the tro-tro had driven off without waiting and there were no more cars in the fort car park, although the streets of Elmina were bustling with business. A smelly hand quickly clamped over Leonard's mouth, the other kids closed in around him, and he was held as tightly as a pig for slaughter. His feet didn't touch the ground as he was hustled past the boats and canoes to the rubbish grounds.

The kids kept him surrounded when they got there. Between two walls of nailed-together crate sides, under a holey corrugated roof, they let Leonard go, and pushed him about.

'Not on the ground! Don' mess his clothes!'

The raggedy band stood in a tight ring. Their mouths fouled him with their insults. Their eyes pierced him like rusty nails. Their hands clawed the air with violent threats. He was at their mercy, crying, shaking, his legs as weak as wheat.

'Let me go! I've got no money! *Please!* You can have my stuff!' He tugged at his school shirt, pointed to his trainers. 'I want my dad…!'

'Listen!' The main boy came over to him. Up close, Leonard could smell the breath that comes from an empty stomach. 'You ain't not got this dad person! Not no more. You ain't not got no one 'cepting this boy –' he thumped his own hollow chest – 'an' this boy, an' this boy, an' this boy' an' this boy!' He went round the circle as each of them sullenly closed his eyes or thrust his crutch out or spat on the ground for the roll call. 'This place is where you live –'

'I live in Accra!' Leonard cried.

'You live *here*, you're always livin' here, you're growin' old an' dyin' here! You get that in your skull, an' you trust it for God's truth! I'm your daddy, he's your mammy, this lot's your uncles an' aunties, we's all your fam'ly. An' we's your bosses!'

The tribal cuts on this daddy's cheek showed that he didn't come from here. The 'mammy', who was the tallest, sniggered and blew Leonard a disgusting kiss. And the most forward of the 'uncles' and 'aunties' growled, 'An' we's your teachers – we surely are gonna learn you!' And they all laughed.

Leonard let out the loudest wail in the world, and his legs finally gave way: his legs, and his consciousness. In a heap on the ground, he didn't hear the final words. 'You been sold to us by Big Fat Chance, pretty little smart boy!'

❀ ❀ ❀

Stephen Boameh was getting cross in his small hotel room up-country in Bonwire. He'd let his mobile phone run down, and the weak call he'd managed to get through received a 'call failed' message as if the line was busy – and Stephen Boameh's home phone line was never busy, except when he was there, or ringing in.

Who was on the line? Doctor? Hospital? The hotel wanting to tell him about some new job? While his mobile phone charged, he lay on his bed and watched a football match on a blinky television screen; but his mind wouldn't settle. He was finished with work for the day. The car had diesel in the tank, oil in the engine, air in the tyres, and water and screen wash all ready for the morning. But if anyone had asked him the score in the match playing up there on a bracket near the ceiling, he couldn't tell them. He couldn't even have said which teams they were.

That morning at the hotel, a photographer and her husband from Scotland had asked about hiring a car to go north. Euros, pounds or American dollars make visitors seem like millionaires in Ghana. So Mr and Mrs Paterson had hired Stephen and his car to take them north to the Kente weaving villages, where the woman wanted to photograph the patterns and the process. This was why Stephen kept his car bright and shiny. With his holdall in the boot he was ready for however many days and nights he might be away. Nana and Leonard understood this. It was his job. The one certain thing, though, was that Stephen would phone every night to talk to Leonard. He never missed. He might be early, he might be late, but some time before Leonard went to sleep he always heard his father's voice.

Tonight was going to be one of those late times. Stephen never used expensive hotel phones, so tonight he had to wait until his mobile charged. But Leonard was on holiday, so a late call wouldn't be the problem it would be in term time.

He fretted, though. He fretted.

These street kids were too poor for drugs. Cheap drink was what they went to sleep on, if they could get it – and tonight they couldn't. While two of them held Leonard down on a stuffed-out mattress, the others scavenged the rubbish tip for food. And when they came back with stale bread, and chicken bones with meagre meat still on them, they shared what there was between them. They were an outlaw band, but disciplined in their own hard way.

Terrified, Leonard took nothing – he would have thrown up. His body was numbed with the loss of all hope. His eyes stared emptily, his mouth dried out. What those boys had said! *No more Dad! No more Nana! No more home!* He shivered and cringed, wept and snivelled, as he tried to imagine what they planned to do with him.

He'd heard about the sort of things people did. It was men with girls, mostly, but it could be with boys. He blanked it from his mind. He just had to watch every move, listen to everything that was said, make himself as small as possible – and run if he could.

Except that the mammy and the uncle were holding him down, with no chance of even getting up. And they were looking at him with eyes like killer wolves.

❀ ❀ ❀

Stephen Boameh shot off the bed and cracked his head when his mobile phone rang. The call was from his mother, Leonard's nana. Her voice was high and shrill.

'Stephen – you didn't take Leonard with you?' she screeched down the phone. 'Is that boy with you?'

'No! Why? *What?*' Stephen kicked his feet free from the mosquito net.

'He's not come in! He went out this morning some time when I was cleaning, and he's not come home…'

'It's eleven o'clock!'

'I've been trying to get you! I never know where you are till you phone us!'

Stephen Boameh would probably remember the curtains in this hotel bedroom for ever, marked all over with the hotel name. He stared at them, unblinking, as he took in this gut-punch news.

'No friends came round for him, no … *people* … about?'

'None that I saw. Stephen, son, you've got to come home!'

'I'm coming! Look for his Day Book, see if there are phone numbers there for school friends – and you ring them, don't mind the time.'

'And the police?'

'When I get there. But ring the Korle-Bu hospital, ask about… road accidents…'

'I've done that. And the Trust hospital, and the Ridge. None with children, they're saying…'

'I'm getting home, fast as I can.'

'Yes, son – really fast! And keep that mobile on!'

Quickly, Stephen telephoned the town's posher hotel where his passengers were staying – nice people who fully understood why he was leaving them. He threw some cedies at the night

desk and ran out with his holdall to the car –
to drive south as he'd never driven before
in his life.

# Chapter Four

Leonard would never let himself go to sleep again. When whatever was going to happen happened, he was going to be awake to fight it; on this he was determined. He wasn't a tough boy, he was more like his father. If people said to Leonard Boameh, *Do you want a fight?* he'd say *No!* and he'd back off. But he wasn't a coward: he didn't think of himself as chicken: he just wasn't aggressive. If he *had* to fight for something, he would. And if he had to fight for his life tonight – or for anything else – he'd fight until his last breath and the last drop of his blood.

Unless he could escape first. But he had no

plan. He wasn't tied up, and no one was sitting on him any more, but when the street kids had finished swearing and smoking and making their backside noises, he was pushed away in a corner furthest away from the curtain of old sacks in the doorway. To get out, he would have to fly like a mosquito over their bodies – unless every one of these kids was asleep; and whenever he lifted his head to look around, there were always night eyes glinting back at him, wide open.

And the uncle had changed his message. Now he sort of smiled, 'C'n jus' kill you!'

'You get yourself to sleep, boy!' the daddy kid croaked, then gave him a kick when Leonard looked around once too often. 'You gotta look real angel boy tomorrow.' And Leonard's numbness came back to cover him like an icy shroud. So, why would he have to look the angel boy tomorrow? Were these kids going to sell him off as a nice-looking little house-boy for someone? Were they going to trade him to someone for

for cedies or dollars? Were they heading over the border with him to Ivory Coast, to sell him off to another people? He'd never get back from that – no one ever did.

He lay there with his eyes staring up, one small tight body in this huddle of tight bodies, except that these others were free...

❀ ❀ ❀

On the road south there seemed to be more stretches of pothole and broken surface than good tarmac, but at this time of night there were no lorries and no street vendors standing at the roadsides holding out their fruit or small meat, so Stephen pushed his old Vauxhall to the limits in his race home. Normally, with passengers poking their cameras out of his windows, or asking this or that about people's lives, and the state of the country, and the flash floods, and the road-building programme, this journey would take him over three hours. Tonight he did it in two; and at just after one o'clock in the morning he yanked on his brake and ran into the house.

And there was Nana's crying face, her head shaking a great big 'No!'

'He's not –?'

'He's not anywhere! Nothing to tell.'

'Not anywhere?' Stephen was rushing into his son's bedroom, looking for some clue, some hope – perhaps a naughty boy's note saying he was going for a sleepover somewhere. But Nana was right: there was nothing; the bed was made up and the cupboard tops tidy.

Stephen pulled the sheet off the bed. Was there a note under there, perhaps?

'I've looked there! I've looked every blessed where. I've telephoned people, telephoned the hospitals…' But Nana threw open cupboards again, rather than standing idle.

Stephen ran out of the room and telephoned 191; and, because of the time of the night, it wasn't long before a police motorcycle came revving up to his door. And within three minutes of hearing about the missing boy, the policeman was on his radio getting a negative response from police headquarters; and within two minutes of that, he was asking the questions every policeman asks: the one that Stephen and Nana had not asked themselves.

'Any money missing?'

They checked. The household money was where it should be.

'What about the boy? Any pocket money?' The policeman's face was hard. He was used to situations such as this.

Stephen ran back into Leonard's bedroom and reached for the wooden pot sitting on a top shelf among a line of small football trophies. His fingers felt in it, around its empty sides. And his look said everything. The boy had taken his money and gone off somewhere.

'Then it looks to me like he's gone of his own free will,' the policeman said. 'You been beatin' him, or there's some other bitterness in him?'

'No!' cried Stephen.

'I swear by our sweet Lord Jesus, that boy gets all the loving any boy could get, from his daddy, and from me...' Nana fell to her knees and started praying: '*Loving Jesus, bring us back our boy...*'

'We got no problems,' Stephen assured the policeman. 'I'm away a lot – I was tonight, driven down from Bonwire; but the boy an' me, we're...' And only now did Stephen Boameh start to cry, pointing at a recent photograph of the pair of them laughing in Kakum National Park.

'Relatives?' the policeman asked, impassive. 'Aunts, uncles ... *mother*?' He eyed Stephen hard. 'Has he run off to his mother?'

Stephen's face came out of his hands. 'She passed on some years back...'

The policeman was unmoved. 'No favourite friends?' Stephen shook his head.

'Then I'll log this. But I guess you better start lookin' round your own circle, man. He has not been abducted.'

'You want a photograph?' Stephen asked, going off to find a recent school portrait in Nana's bedroom.

'Can, if you like.'

With fumbling fingers, Stephen took the photograph out of its frame, deliberately not looking at his smiling boy in school uniform.

Now the policeman unbent a fraction. 'Nice-looking kid!' he said. He tucked the photograph carefully into his pocket book, but he wrote down the details of Leonard's name, date of birth and the school shirt he was wearing just as a matter of routine. As far as he was concerned, the kid had run away from home.

❀ ❀ ❀

Leonard thought they were all asleep. He must have drifted off himself for a bit, because he was suddenly woken up by a mosquito whining round his head. But he didn't dare open his eyes straight off; he gave it a few moments, then

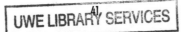

opened them as if his eyelids might make a noise. He hooded his stare so that his eyes wouldn't glint, but the stubs of candles stuck on nails had gone out and the place was dark, except for the glow of an oil drum fire flickering through the weave of the sack curtain. He listened intently. Surrounding him was snoring, and muttering, and the grinding of teeth; and in the distance he could hear the never-ending roar of the sea. Elmina was deep in its night.

Leonard knew what he was going to do. It must have come to him in whatever sleep he'd had, because the plan was there, complete in his mind, when he woke. He knew it would be no good wriggling up and trying to tiptoe his trainers between these sleeping bodies – everyone was too tightly packed together. Softly-softly was the wrong approach.

But what if he jumped up as fast as he could and ran across the bodies to the doorway, throwing himself out of it before anyone knew what was happening? Surprise – the direct way!

The *only* way – he knew that. Some people slept soundly, like Nana, others lightly, like his dad, who would shoot up in bed the second Leonard approached his door. And there would be light sleepers in this hell-band of kids too.

Yes, that's what he would do… He lay there and his muscles rehearsed the escape. He tensed his elbows for the first lift-up, and his thighs for the knee-bend, and his legs for the straightening as he stood up; and in his mind he pumped his arms as he ran over the kids' bodies to that glow behind the sacking. He relaxed his muscles, then found that he'd held his breath too long, and had to let it out slowly so as not to make a loud sighing noise. He kept his mouth shut, breathed in through his nostrils, and built up his lungs again, like an athlete going for the high jump. He was still lying flat, but now with the smallest wriggle he lifted his body for action, tensed his muscles again.

He listened for the final time. It was still all snoring, and muttering, and grinding – and distant sea beckoning him with the sound of freedom.

He counted in his head. One, two, *three!* And suddenly his muscles did what they'd rehearsed. He elbowed, he pushed, he stood, and he ran ducking for the sack doorway, over the bodies of the street kids…

…To fall flat on his front as he trod on the first body, landing with a thump across the sleeping forms – which weren't sleeping any more, but roused, and shouting, and cursing and hitting out at this object that had crashed across them.

But it was the uncle who was widest awake. 'One more time – an' we kill you!' And because he'd been hurt, he kicked up angrily at Leonard. Leonard was pushed back to his place, buffeted there, and left crying and calling for his dad.

But it was his new daddy who answered him. 'We tied your shoe laces, Angel Boy! We ain't chicken brains!'

In a new snivel of fear, Leonard lay flat, exhausted, not even able to defeat the mosquito that had been plaguing him all night.

# Chapter Five

Before dawn, Stephen Boameh was at the quarries north of Accra. Whenever he drove visitors out of the capital, he did his best to avoid this area, where child labour was at its worst. Here infants as young as three could be seen breaking up stone for the roads and for concrete. Sometimes it was their parents, the adults, breaking up the large stones, stacked in piles for the youngsters to break into medium stones, with the really young children sitting on top of the piles to hammer them into small pieces.

But sometimes – and everyone knew this –

the children were abducted from poor neighbourhoods to do the work. Children who go missing in Ghana don't take up any newspaper space, they're not part of any story that sells.

When the sight of a toddler breaking stones at the roadside couldn't be avoided, Stephen told his passengers that *Children in Need Ghana* was doing something about the problem, but with a rub of his fingers he'd bemoan the fact that commerce and money are always more powerful than charity work.

Early that morning, the quarries were the first places that he searched. But as the sun rose and the dust-covered families and the children on their own arrived in flaps and tatters of grey, there was no sign of Leonard. In his red school shirt he would have stood out like a bright flag – unless, of course, it had been ripped off his back.

Stephen drove along all the roadworks where he knew that re-surfacing was going on. He parked time after time, was shouted and sworn at by overseers. He drove and drove, his eyes lighting up with any flash of red; he went back into Makola Market, where a jostle of buyers threaded through tight streets of shops and stalls, and he walked on to the shanty town beside the sea. But nowhere was there any sign of Leonard Boameh. He telephoned Nana every fifteen minutes, but the moment she answered him, the tone of her voice told him what he dreaded to hear. No word. It was as if his son had vanished off the face off the earth.

❀ ❀ ❀

In Elmina's shanty town, the boys were getting Leonard ready. One of his aunties brought a chipped enamel bowl of sea water. *What was this?* He soon found out. Two of them forced him to kneel, and another two grabbed his head and ducked him under the water. He fought, but he was held tightly, and quickly brought out. This was to wash the soot and cinders out of his hair. He was made to stand up, and the uncle rubbed the grey off his knees with an old rag. Others pulled the creases out of his Blessed Wisdom top while his shorts had the dust smacked out of them, back and front, which hurt badly.

'Yeah!' His tall mammy looked down at him. 'A real angel boy!'

Leonard's insides churned with the fear of the condemned. He tried to be brave, he tried to stand up tall, the way he would for the stick at school, he thought of his dad and his nana and the Lord Jesus, and he tried to say a prayer – but he couldn't find any holy words, just 'Help me!' His mouth was as dry as the ever-drifting smoke, his eyes smarted, but they wouldn't clear because he was cried out.

'What you gotta do…' – the tribal-cut leader was up close again – 'you gotta be polite, an' the laughing-boy, an' more nicer than the student kids…' Leonard frowned, concentrating. Even in his fear, he had to learn what might keep him alive.

'The conch-shell boys, the college kids…'

Suddenly Leonard realised what he meant. The smart-looking boys he'd seen were students. Now he knew why they'd been so much cleaner than these street kids: hadn't his dad told him about the Accra boys who, like them, were looking for sponsors to pay for their education?

'We don' get to take nothin' when them college kids is at the fort. But *you* can. You stand up by the entrance above them, an' you smile in your smart school shirt, an' you ask people all polite for dollars. You got me?'

Leonard nodded, while inside he heaved a great sigh of relief. He wasn't going to be killed, or sold across the border to another country. He wasn't going to be taken off and have nasty stuff done to him.

He was going to have to beg.

'We kill you!' the uncle reminded him. 'We're near, an' you say one word or you try to run…' and he kicked Leonard hard in the groin. The kick doubled Leonard over, made him want to vomit, the empty pain rolling deep down.

'You got that?' The mammy pulled him up by his hair.

Leonard managed a nod.

'We're nice as your ol' mammy when you know us. An' we're your family now.' The daddy rubbed his fingers together. 'So you get lots o' dollars, right? We eat top tonight.' And his belly rumbled.

Everyone stared at Leonard.

Leonard nodded again.

'What's your name?'

'Leonard. Leonard Boameh.'

The daddy grinned at him. 'You *was* Leonard Boameh!' He made it sound like Ashanti royalty. 'Now you "Angel Boy". You got that?'

Leonard stared at the ground. Even his name was being stolen from him.

'*What* your name?' the mammy asked.

It took Leonard a few seconds to say it, beating another groin-kick by just a vowel. 'Angel Boy,' he said.

They whooped and cheered, and spat, and

punched the air as if they'd won some prize.

'Right, Angel Boy, we's goin' to work!' And in the same tight formation that had brought him there, Leonard was hustled off the rubbish tip, past the boats and the harbour, through the fort car park, and up beyond the staring conch students to the gate of the fort – where the uncle hid beyond him in a small hollow in the ground.

The other street kids slouched down the slope towards the car park, trading insults with the conch students, and as the sun rose higher everyone waited for the tourists to come, with Leonard standing there like a tethered goat.

❋ ❋ ❋

Leonard's father drove to the Blessed Wisdom Primary School, but the gates were locked and there was no sign of the caretaker. He shouted through into the yard, but there was nothing going on inside the building – no cleaning, no maintenance work.

He drove back to the Nile Hotel, where the owner heard his terrible story and did all she could to help him. On her office computer they scanned a photograph of Leonard, and made it into a poster for a missing boy: and she generously offered to make the reward offered for his return a lot bigger.

Stephen toured the Cantonment District with the posters, pinning them to trees, asking for display space in the cafés and bars and money exchanges; and showing them to the kids selling plantain chips and ice water at the crossroads.

Finally, not knowing what else to do, he drove the streets and walked the alleys of Accra, peering at people for a sighting of Leonard's familiar face. Then, dispirited, he ended up in the Cathedral of the Holy Spirit, and lit a candle, and bowed his head in prayer for the safe return of his son.

# Chapter Six

The tourists came past the conch students in different moods. If they had read the better guide books they brushed past, keeping strong grips on their cameras and bags. Others, like the backpackers the day before, gave their names to the boys with good humour. Either way, by the time they had walked up the slope to where Leonard was standing, the visitors were relieved to be free of hassle.

And then they reached Leonard: a smart boy, younger, short-trousered, with big appealing eyes

– straight out of a television advertisement. But in truth, while Leonard's mouth was appealing for money, his eyes were appealing for help.

'Please give to my school. We're buying footballs and books. We want to read, and we want to be sportsmen.' Leonard remembered the last Blessed Wisdom appeal and held out the clean china plate that the daddy had given him – stolen from some café.

'Which school is that, fellah?' a big white American asked him.

'The Blessed Wisdom Primary, sir.' He pointed to the holy cross on his pocket.

'You're short of readers and footballs?'

'And paper… and gospels, sir.' Now, since that first lie to the tro-tro people, Leonard was getting good at making things up.

'Your teachers know you're doing this?' The woman was American, too, and black. 'This collectin' plate has gotten their per-mission?'

'Yes, ma'am.' Leonard nodded into the fort. 'The teachers do guiding and selling in the…

tour places… while the students do this. For extra money.'

The small group of tourists looked at one another; and the man pulled out his wallet to place an American ten dollar bill on the plate.

'Enjoy your reading and your sport, fellah,' he said. 'But make sure the ball's not a round one…' And, laughing at his American football joke, he followed the others to the fort entrance.

It had been that easy. Leonard looked down at the green bill on the plate. He'd begged ten dollars!

'Put a thumb on it!' came the uncle's voice from its little hollow. 'Show it!'

Already, another small cluster of tourists was coming towards the entrance. Leonard's father would have recognised them straight off as English, in their samey frocks and safari shirts.

'Good morning!' Leonard bowed. 'God bless you. This is a collection for my school. The Blessed Wisdom Primary. We're saving up for books and different-shaped balls, and paper, and gospels…'

There was a cough and a spit from the hollow and Leonard realised he was overdoing it.

'A school collection?' a real boss-aunty Englishwoman asked. 'Have you got a licence for a charity day?'

'Yes, ma'am.' Leonard looked up to the sky with his most 'little angel' face. He suddenly thought of his father's car number plate. 'GT6093H, the teacher's got the paper.' And he waved his hand vaguely towards the fort. 'Stamped with the date,' he added, 'by the judge…'

There was another impatient cough from the hollow, and the woman frowned at Leonard. 'That sounds like a car number plate!' she said. '*That* sort of licence.'

But a younger woman stepped up, smiling. 'Well, if it was, he deserves something for being a resourceful young boy. Life isn't easy out here.' And she put a pocketful of scruffy cedies on to the plate. 'Don't spend it all at once!'

Leonard bowed as they went on into the fort with the rest of their group. He stuffed the cedies into his pocket, leaving the American bill alone on the plate. It looked more enticing that way. And with a worm of conscience, he realised that for a few moments he had half-forgotten who he was, what he was, and what he was standing here doing. He was a captive beggar of some street kids who were going to keep him as one of their gang. He was homeless, an orphan. And this was his job from now on…

A babble of noise distracted him. Coming up the slope was a big party of students, some white, some black, about twenty in all, with a tall bald man in charge, and a younger woman further back. They were all wearing rucksacks and they were walking and talking, some treading backwards, others jumping at one another in their eager conversations. The sound was like a landing of noisy gulls, as if Elmina Fort was just another clipboard stop on a school tour.

Leonard stood in front of the teacher. 'Good

morning, sir,' he said.

'*Au revoir, monsieur!*' the man replied, looking down at him like a general. '*Dépêche-toi!*' His hand waved Leonard away, and the river of French students engulfed him.

Leonard was surrounded. Surrounded! And he suddenly realised that he could no longer be seen among all these legs and bags – even by the lurking uncle. Keeping himself hidden tight among them, Leonard shuffled with the French party up to the fort entrance. And within moments, in the throng of the pay office area, the teacher waved a permit at the cashier and the whole group was ushered through into the fort. The entry door was shut behind them: Leonard still in their midst – in a place where the *We kill you!* uncle outside couldn't follow him!

What to do? Who to tell? Leonard knew that he had a little time on his side, but who would believe him, who would take action to help him?

Immediately, he thought: the teacher! Not the Frenchman, but the young woman guide who worked here. She would remember him from yesterday.

'*Asseyez-vous. On attends le guide!*' the French teacher shouted to the students.

Leonard understood that; his father had clients from all over Europe, spoke some French himself. The French party was going to have to sit and wait for the guide to finish the tour she was currently taking round.

The students sat and filled the fort with their noise, rummaging in their rucksacks for snacks, while Leonard quickly ran into the courtyard. Facing him was the church; to his left were the male and female slave dungeons, to his right the condemned cell, and straight ahead, down the steps, was the Door of No Return. The Americans and the English were somewhere in there, being shown round by the guide he needed to find. So where were they? Where was she?

He listened hard for a female voice; it was difficult to hear above the babble of the French, especially since she had a soft voice.

He looked this way and that, peered into the darkness of the dungeons, and, suddenly, there was the group, coming out of the church. And with them was the guide.

*But it was not the young woman from yesterday!* This morning the guide was a biggish man, already moving people on quickly, too many visitors, too much to do, not looking at all sympathetic. And he certainly wouldn't remember Leonard, because he'd never seen him before.

Swiftly, Leonard ran to the kindest person in the group: the American who'd made the joke about the footballs. 'Please, sir…' he said.

'Not you again!'

'Please, sir, I'm in trouble –'

'Not another cent, fellah!'

'It's not about that, it's not about school!'

'It never was!' the older Englishwoman said. 'He's giving us one cock-and-bull story after another!'

'But this is true! I've been kidnapped!

Captured! Those kids have made me their prisoner!'

The black American woman grabbed hold of Leonard's shirt by the collar. 'Listen, boy! We ain't took in!' She shook him, like Nana with a dirty mat. 'Them clean an' tidy students outside, they're decent kids, they just ain't that sort to kidnap anyone –'

'Not them. The other ones!' Now Leonard was being held up on his toes.

'Rubbish!' the Englishwoman poked in. 'You're trying it on, sonny-boy! And we've had enough of it – want, want, want, wherever we go!'

Even her kind niece was shaking her head at this wicked child. But the American woman hadn't finished with Leonard. She still hadn't let him go. 'I'm here for my ancestors! I'm here to pay my respects. I've made the trip from a fam'ly line of African slaves, and I'm the first of the line to be priv'liged to return. And I'm not having this *sig-nif-icant* moment spoiled by a beggar brat!

Now get off my sidewalk!'

She let Leonard go with a push, almost propelling him into the hands of the big frowning guide who was coming at him, reaching out his hands.

But up near the entrance was the French group. 'My friends!' Leonard said, hoping that the guide hadn't taken in too much of what the others had said. 'I go! *Au revoir!*' He dodged the man's hands and backed off towards the French sounds.

'What did I tell you!' the old Englishwoman said. 'Never trust anyone!'

Out of immediate reach, Leonard hovered. If he wasn't careful, he was going to be back where he'd started with the street kids, who knew they couldn't trust him an inch. If they let him live, they'd teach him a harsh lesson first. But no one in here was going to listen to him. So what could he do? Where could he go? It was no good walking towards the French party, because he'd already tried begging from them.

And, as if in some sort of answer, an idea came to him. As soon as the tourist group had been led on their way, he peeled off from the fort entrance and ran into the church. Churches have pews, good for hiding behind, and no one visiting Elmina Fort came in here for long – not with those dungeons and that dramatic door outside – unless it was to pray. And people praying have all their attention fixed on God.

So the church was a good place to be right now, for a small soul hiding in a dark corner…

# Chapter Seven

Leonard curled himself up into a ball at the back of the church, behind a curtain where it looked as if they kept the sort of stuff that wasn't wanted every day: broken chairs, a bent and tarnished altar rail, and a dusty picture of the crucified Jesus.

He didn't know what time it was. Groups had come in, and groups had gone. Some had lingered a bit longer than others, but no one had stayed long enough to wander around.

It was getting dark now, and after a long spell with no one coming in, Leonard reckoned that the visitors must have gone for the day. But he wasn't coming out. He had found a good place here, and although he imagined he could hear voices hissing, *We kill you! Get that, Angel Boy!* he realised that it was the sound of the wind in the battlements; and the distant shouting in his ears wasn't the street kids, but the boat-builders and footballers down below on the beach.

Night falls fast in Ghana, and it was dark within minutes. Now what? He could stay here until morning and try and get help from some fresh visitors who hadn't seen him begging. He could hang about in the hope that tomorrow was the kind young woman's day to be the guide again. Or he could try to get out of this place in the middle of the night.

But what about the street kids? Would they have given up on him? Would they be moving on to some other evil plan to get money? Or were they the sort to cling to something, to see it through to the end if it gave them a small chance to earn big money like ten dollar bills?

*Ten dollar bills!* Suddenly Leonard realised that he still had one.

He'd left the collecting plate on a stone seat in the fort entrance-way, but he still had the money. It would get him a taxi home if he managed to get out of here! He felt it crinkle in his top pocket. As for the cedies in his shorts, they wouldn't even get him a bag of plantain chips – which made him realise how hungry he was. His stomach rolled emptily and he was startled by its loudness. He was thirsty, too, but like a mouse he was going to have to lie low until later.

The fort was dark. There were offices here, and a museum, but not a chink of light was to be seen. If there was a caretaker, he or she probably lived down in the town. Leonard had the feeling that he was all alone..

He had to be patient, though. As the heat of the day went out of the timbers, the woodwork started to creak; and every creak sounded like a stealthy footstep…The street kids? Could one of them have wormed into the fort and right now be prowling the place looking for 'Angel Boy'? Leonard's eyes were as big as a civet cat's, his ears as sensitive as a radio telescope as he held his breath to listen and moved the curtain to look around. Who else was in this place?

He stayed where he was – and sitting there, hunched and hiding in the church recess, another scary thought seeped into Leonard's mind. *Slaves. Ghosts. The spirits of the people who had been locked up in the fort to die in the condemned cell.* In his head he saw the sculpted skull above the cell's entrance, and he imagined its hollow sockets staring through the dark of the night, even through the walls…

He believed in Jesus, and the badge on his school shirt said he believed in the Holy Ghost. But what about *people* ghosts? What about those forebears who had died metres away from where he sat? Were their spirits free at night to escape from that locked dungeon of death?

He had to get out of here!

Carefully, he pushed the recess curtain aside.

It squeaked on its rail, made enough noise to wake a million spirits – but he pushed himself through, and out he came into the vaulted air of the nave. He could see better here – there was a moon. It filtered in through the glass, and let him see his way to the church door.

*Please God it wasn't locked!* And it wasn't. A turn on the ring handle and he stepped out into the moon-wash of the courtyard. He kept his eyes away from the dungeons and the condemned cell, and to bring good luck he crossed himself the way the Catholics do, before running under the archway to the fort entrance. There was just a chance that it was only bolted from the inside, and he could slide the bolts.

Some chance! As he walked towards it, squinting his eyes now that he was out of the moonshine again, he saw the big entrance door with security locks as well as bolts. He tried it just in case – and as he looked through the crack, his body froze. Outside sat a street kid, the leader, the tribal-cut daddy. His head lifted from his chest as the door rattled.

*Oh, no!*

Leonard scuttled away from the door. *They were waiting for him! They knew he was still in here!* He turned and ran back into the courtyard. His stomach rolled with fear. He ran beyond the courtyard on to the battlements where cannon balls were heaped behind a line of black cannons, pointing out to sea. He went to the ramparts and stared down. And there on the rocks beneath him were two more street kids, crouching and staring silently up at him. His stomach seemed to eat his heart.

Leonard Boameh had never felt so alone in his life. Shivering on the ramparts of Elmina Castle, he looked at the heavens – but he didn't see God; he saw the same stars and moon that are forever blind to human suffering. And he crumpled. He collapsed there on the worn flagstones, and sobbed.

*But there was another exit from this place!* There was the Door of No Return! Could that be

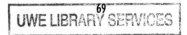

opened from the inside without a key? And would the patrolling street kids be watching it? He pulled himself up from the flagstones and made his way, stooping, to the infamous door, pressing himself tight against the wall. He stared at the doorway. Its shape was hard to see against the moonlight sea, but there it was, firmly closed, its stunted bars letting just a glimmer of light in – and so small that only a cat could get through.

There was no street kid beyond it, up at this level. There might be one waiting below – but for now, it was safe to try the door.

It was locked. Of course it was locked. And although Leonard tried his head for size – because where a head and shoulders can go, don't they say the body can follow? – there was no way that even a skinny kid could get out through here.

He stood back. This way was hopeless, too; which meant there would be only one time to get out, and that was when people were around. Tomorrow. But how could he do that, with the fort guarded by the street kids? Even if he jumped from the battlements without breaking his legs or his neck, they would get him. He sank down on his haunches as he realised that these kidnappers were not going to give up on him. That rotten ten dollar bill had proved that he was a brother worth having...

# Chapter Eight

Leonard spent the night behind the pyramid of cannonballs furthest from the fort entrance. Desperate to keep awake, he leant uncomfortably against them and tried to work out what to do. His one big hope would be that the young woman guide would be on duty the next day. She would listen and she would help him. If that didn't work, he could try walking out of the fort with the visitors and dodging the waiting street kids, or persuade tourists of the trouble he was in. But would they be able to listen to him if the short-fuse guide was around? There was one

72

other skinny hope – that a different guide altogether would be on duty tomorrow – but he was just going to have to find out.

❋ ❋ ❋

Next morning, the sun woke the seabirds first, terns *krik-krikking* in the distance, and the gulls screeching down where the fishing boats came in. Then light, rather than warmth, woke Leonard, who had slid into a fitful sleep despite himself. He stretched, remembered with a slam of his hopes where he was, then shut his eyes again so as not to look at the light coming straight at him. And as he opened his eyes to stare at the shadowed ramparts, he saw the sun's after-image on his retina almost as clearly as the sun itself, blinding him to the stonework before him.

And suddenly he had an idea. Where had that retina thing happened before? Not long ago. Where had he been blinded for a while, and what had he seen instead? It was where there were bars, a pattern of bright bars in a rectangle.

His hyped-up brain quickly gave him the answer. It had been at the Door of No Return, where the light through the bars that first day had been so intense that he hadn't seen the two backpackers standing against the walls beside it.

So couldn't someone else standing there be invisible too – until they could mingle in with the rest of the group? Couldn't he make himself invisible for a vital few moments?

Yes! That's what he could do! If he could keep himself unnoticed and uncounted until that gate-door was opened, he could run out and get down to the beach.

*So long as no street kids were still waiting for him!*

But it was his best chance – although Leonard knew that wasn't saying much; not much at all.

❊ ❊ ❊

Stephen Boameh had spent a day fruitlessly searching for his son; and on the second morning he was up at dawn to check the quarries and the roadworks again. But he saw nobody new, just the same overseers who had shouted him away the previous day.

He telephoned the hospitals, and he telephoned the police; he telephoned the Blessed Wisdom Primary School, and he telephoned the homes of the friends from Leonard's school whose numbers he could find. But he drew the same blanks as before. Nobody had heard anything about his boy.

Nana wasn't singing hymns today. She hadn't been singing them the day before, either. Instead, she was praying. Her eyes when they were open were on the telephone; and her eyes when they were closed were on the picture of Jesus that she carried in her head – with him saying, 'Suffer the little children to come unto me.'

Every time the telephone rang she jumped like someone scalded. But there was no news. And as the first day and night ran into the second day and night, and the third morning dawned, her thoughts and those of Leonard's father began to take a sinister turn.

Was Leonard never to be heard of again?

❀ ❀ ❀

Leonard waited silently against the wall by the doorway. From where he was standing, everything was bright and focused in the light coming through the bars of the Door of No Return. But his memory and his senses told him that it wasn't the same the other way round. For a while he would be invisible to the visitors.

As he heard the first party coming round the fort, the voice told him the identity of the guide. It was the big man who had tried to grab him the day before. Leonard's pleasant young woman had let him down: she wasn't at work today; and his skin-thin hope shrivelled.

He was now standing where the deepest shadow seemed to be; near enough to the door for the contrast to be strong – bright sunshine and deep darkness – but not so close that the light spilled on to his body. He stood, and he waited; he knew from before that once the tourist party was in the courtyard, it would be about fifteen minutes before they reached him, before all their eyes were staring at that terrible door. He stood as still as he could. And he wondered if his school shirt might be too bright, even in the darkness; so he took it off. He held it behind him, and he waited, and waited...

At last they came.

'Here we're comin' to the in-famous Door of No Return...' This man didn't have the quiet, reverent sympathy of the young woman.

'Jus' down by here...'

It was a good-sized group, about fifteen of them, a mixed pick-up from the entrance. They came shuffling and focusing their cameras into the small space – a squeeze for camera-carrying tourists, but big enough in its day for slave-stripping and branding.

'Here was where they wen' out, an' never

come back.' The guide unlocked the door with a key from his pocket. 'These are the steps they were taken down.' He stood aside to let the group see, their eyes hooded against the bright sun.

Some took photographs, some stood still, some touched the bars, some stepped outside – and, unseen, Leonard slid away from the wall, tried to mingle among the visitors and, seeing a space between two photographers whose eyes were focused on their lenses, he made his move. If he could just squeeze between –

*Boy!'* The guide growled like a mastiff and grabbed at Leonard. 'You back here, are you?'

People stopped, they turned or twisted – which was just movement enough for Leonard to slip between two tourists and go head-down for the doorway. The guide grabbed at him again, but only got his shirt – and Leonard was away, jumping down the rough steps to the beach. His eyes were on the stones, and they were everywhere else for a sight of one of the street kids.

He leapt from the bottom step and ran on sand, then gravel and then grass as he raced to where the fishing boats clustered, where men and boys were sorting the morning catch, all sweat and nets. He was grateful not to be in his shirt, because he didn't stand out, he was just one more bare-skinned boy by the boats. But without the money in its pocket any more.

He turned to look back at the fort. And what he saw sank him as if he were running over shifting sand. Two street kids, the father and the tall, fast mother, were sprinting after him across the grass shouting, 'Stop! Angel Boy! Stop!'

Leonard ran even faster. He wove between the boats, he jumped a mound of nets, he cracked a shin hard on a crate of fish, and he made for the houses up beyond the football pitch. If he could knock at someone's door…

But they were cutting him off. A quick look round told him that the street kids knew where he was heading. The tall one was running to his left and would get him as he came out from between the boats.

Like a trapped roebuck, Leonard turned, ducked back, thought of heading for the sea and swimming; but he'd be exposed out there – and these kids from Elmina would have grown up swimming. As he ran, he stooped so as to be less easily seen, skinning himself between boats and fishermen and nets.

He took a last desperate chance. On the water's edge was a bigger fishing boat, with empty nets lying jumbled in the prow. He grazed his belly slithering over the boat's side and crabbed himself awkwardly under the black nets.

There he lay, taking great gulps of fishy air. He balled himself as tight as a boy could, his head on the bottom planks of the boat, smelling the sea-salty wood. He muttered the prayer he hadn't been able to call up the night before:

*Our Father, which art in heaven…*

How long? How long would it be before they found him? They knew where he wasn't, so they must know where he was. It would only be minutes before they came through the boats and searched him out. He told himself he was in for a beating and a yank back to the street-kid life – if they didn't kill him instead...

'Angel Boy! Angel Boy!' His heart stood still as he heard them getting nearer. 'We's comin'! We's goin' to find you, Angel Boy!'

## Chapter Nine

The voices were close by. The kids were only seconds away from pulling up the mound of net and finding him. Above the voices of fishermen he heard hands grabbing and scrabbling at the sides of the boat he was in – and now, with a stomach-lurch, he felt the rocking of the vessel, and the movement in her. They were here! Getting in!

'Angel Boy! We's got you!'

He knocked his head in the sudden push of the boat, and a pick-up of motion – and a great drenching through the nets before there was a different sort of movement, like the swell of a wave.

Suddenly Leonard realised. The boat had put out to sea. He pulled the net away from his face to look around him, and saw two muscular men oaring, one steering in the stern, and two others coming towards him for the nets.

'What you doin' here, boy?' The first was big and gruff, like the guide from the fort. The others looked round from their rowing and steering. They tutted, muttered, made noises in their throats. 'You bin stealin' our snapper?'

They looked fierce, they rowed out to sea even faster. He looked pleadingly at them. Would they throw him overboard? Would they hold him under the water and drown him? Did they think he wanted to steal their fish?

'Well, what you doin', scramblin' around these nets?'

Against the slap of the waves and the creak of the boat and the hard rowing, Leonard shouted, 'I ran away from home! But only for the day…'

The man was listening. 'And...?' he said impatiently. 'What then?'

'I've been captured by street kids. They were by the boat – they said I've got to stay with them...'

'Stealin' fish?'

'No! Begging. At the fort.'

The man was bracing himself with strong arms between the two sides of the boat. His muscles looked awesome. Quickly, Leonard told the man his name loud enough to be heard by the other fishermen, and he told them his address and phone number, and everything that had happened to him.

They seemed to be thinking it over. The man near him unscrambled the nets, untwining Leonard's arms and legs and trainers. The others went on rowing and steering, but they shouted out their opinions.

'We got a street kid here with a high tale...'

'No better than the rest. Run off from the quarries...'

*Row, row, row, slap, slap, slap, creak, creak, creak.*
*Mutter, mutter, mutter* – and *spit.*

Leonard was crying again. Nobody in the world believed him. They were going to dump him out at sea, or take him back to the street kids who would be waiting – who knew that he was in this boat.

'Please! Please help me!'

The man with the long steering oar suddenly pulled it in and came along the boat. He was clearly the man in charge. He looked at Leonard's feet. He reached out and twisted one, and stroked its trainer, and nodded, appreciating its good make.

'Your name! Again!' He clicked his fingers into Leonard's face.

'Leonard Stephen Boameh.'

'Where from? Up-country? Cape Coast?'

'Twenty-one Liberation Road, Cantonment District, Accra.'

The man was trying to trick him into making a mistake, because Leonard had said this already.

'Your father name?'

'Stephen Boameh. He drives for the Nile Hotel.'

'The Nile?'

'On Nsawam Road.'

'You go to school?'

'The Blessed Wisdom Primary. Accra.' If only he still had his school shirt!

'You got learnin' then?'

Leonard nodded. 'Some.'

The man rubbed at the stubble on his face, still staring Leonard in the eyes. 'Then you tell me some learnin'.'

Leonard stared back. 'What sort?'

The man shrugged. 'Jus' let me hear you're no urchin – that you got teachin' inside of you…'

Leonard blinked, red light through his eyelids. What could he say? Recite a times table? Go through the countries that made up Africa? Say a psalm? This was the sort of test no one prepared you for in school. But suddenly he heard his own voice against the slapping and the creaking of the boat.

"*The beginning of wisdom is knowing who you are. Draw near and listen.*' That was what the woman guide had said to him at the Door of No Return.

But it wasn't enough. All it did was draw the man nearer to Leonard to listen, as if it had been an instruction. 'Get on with it!'

Leonard's head was blank. It was as if he had never learnt anything. But he had! Where had he been these last days?

'Elmina Fort, St George's Castle, was built in 1482,' he declared, remembering his teacher and the woman guide, who in his head were suddenly rolled into one person. 'Its name – Elmina – comes from the word for "old mine". At first it was where gold and other stuff were traded, until the slave business started. Then millions of slaves were traded instead…'

That should do it – and the man was nodding. But, 'Street kids learn that stuff for tourists,' he said. 'I want real *learnin'* learnin', boy. Proper reciting or scientific facts.'

Leonard didn't know what to say. He couldn't think of any scientific facts. He cast around desperately, shaking his head, but all he could call up right now was Nana's singing, the words of the hymns from her constant wailing. So he quoted her favourite, but tried to say it with meaning, more like a poem he had learned at school.

*"What a friend we have in Jesus,*
*    all our sins and griefs to bear!*
*What a privilege to carry everything to God in prayer!*
*O what peace we often forfeit,*
*O what needless pain we bear,*
*All because we do not carry everything*
*to God in prayer…"*

He winced as he finished, but the helmsman was nodding. Leonard cleared his throat to begin on verse two.

'*Amen!*' the helmsman said. And he rubbed Leonard's head like Nana did when she was pleased with him.

Dear Nana! Dear boring Nana who couldn't dive for the ball when she was in goal. Had she just saved him?

'You ain't no street kid – they never see the insides of a Christian church…' The man turned around and signalled to his crew. 'We're takin' this boy back, we're findin' the p'lice, an' we're returnin' him to his father.'

The other fishermen muttered and moaned, but they turned the boat around and took it back to Elmina Beach, where they pulled it up on to the sand. With a terrible stomach lurch inside, Leonard saw them: the street kids, still there. They must have watched the boat returning, and right now they were hovering near – but not too near – like wolves waiting to strike the weakest calf, but keeping their escape runs open.

Leonard stared at them, and moved closer to the helmsman.

'An' you can lose your sinnin' bodies!' the man shouted at the kids. He lunged towards them, and they ran back a few metres like wolves from a lion.

'You want this boy?' he shouted at them. 'You come to Brekoso police station an' ask the constable for him…'

The street kids watched them go before sloping away. It looked as if they had lost their Angel Boy. But hungry creatures will wait days for their prey. Those hungry street kids hadn't given up yet. Not by a long way had they given up…

# Chapter Ten

The way to Brekoso police station took the fishermen and Leonard through the market, past stacks of fish boxes, skirting the 'Jesus Never Fails' chop house, and along lines of stalls selling everyday goods. This was nothing like Makola Market in Accra, here the three of them could walk abreast – but it was busy enough for the daddy street kid to make a surprise move.

A tall pile of empty fish boxes stood two men high at the side of the walkway. As the fishermen dropped hands with Leonard to weave past the buying and the bartering at the stalls, a sudden push from behind sent the boxes toppling into the aisle – and separated the trio from each other. Everyone went arms-up as twenty or thirty sharp-edged boxes came clattering down.

'*Whoa!*'

'Mind them heads!'

'What fool did that?'

There were angry shouts as everyone looked around – while the daddy kid and two uncles came darting out from behind the stalls and grabbed at Leonard.

He shouted 'Help!' and took off between the stalls. Dodging the grabbing hands he ran, he wove, he jumped boxes and curls of sisal rope as he put down his head and fled.

But one boy was directly behind him, and another was running to cut him off – Leonard could see him from the corner of his eye. A hand from a stall-holder grabbed at the kid following, and held him – releasing him as he twisted, but delaying the chase for vital seconds. At the same moment, a surprise two-storey building blocked the out-runner, giving Leonard a chance to sprint up towards the streets of houses east of the market. But from the shouts and the whoops, he knew his tormentors weren't far away. And he knew that his breath and his strength could never outrun the lot of them.

So he did something either very clever or very crazy. He doubled back. Those fishermen were back there in the market somewhere, and the street kids would still think he was blindly running on and on, away from them. Throwing a quick look back to check that he couldn't be seen, he ran past a large white house and then right around it, doubling back down a parallel alley to where he could sprint towards the market, and the harbour.

Would his quick thinking outwit their faster legs? Tired, scared, grabbed back from safety, Leonard could only pray that it would.

❀ ❀ ❀

Back in Accra, a call came to the Nile Hotel. As the hotel owner lifted the phone from its cradle Stephen Boameh was busy in the office printing more pictures of his son. He hardly looked up; a ringing telephone with no news was what he expected.

But the tone of the hotel owner's voice made him lift his head.

'Yes! Yes!' She was beckoning to Stephen. 'He's right here, you tell him!'

Stephen grabbed the phone from her.

You got a boy…?' the voice over the phone said.

Stephen somehow found breath. 'I got a boy.'

'Leonard… something?'

'Leonard Stephen Boameh.'

'Yeah. What school he goes to…?'

'Blessed Wisdom Primary. Accra.'

'Sounds like. Police here, Elmina, he's been seen. Some fishermen. Found him an' lost him. In a mix-up with street kids…'

Stephen's face showed quick relief and then

fear. 'I'm coming! I'm coming fast!'

'Brekoso police station. You bring a picture of the boy…'

Leonard's father threw down the phone, snatched up a handful of prints and ran out to his car.

'Good luck!' called the hotel owner.

Stephen slammed himself into the Vauxhall. 'Pray for us!' he shouted through the cracked windscreen, before reversing on screeching tyres into Nsawam Road.

❋ ❋ ❋

Leonard was trapped. Within seconds he would be back in the grip of the street kids – who would hide him deep in the shanties until the busy fishermen had forgotten him.

He was running back through the town, not daring to believe that he had outwitted the kids. The trouble was, he didn't know the geography of this place the way he knew his own district.

He suddenly found himself facing the bridge that spanned the harbour entrance. There was no way to the left, no way to the right. He threw a quick look behind him. Nothing. He looked across the bridge. Nothing. So he ran on to cross it, praying that he'd find some sort of hiding-place on the other side. If he lay low up beyond Elmina Castle, perhaps he could make his way back to find the police after darkness came.

He was only halfway across the bridge when he saw it. Like a scare in the night, a figure came springing out from nowhere – the tall street-kid, the fastest runner of them all, his face grimacing around the girders.

*No! Please, no!*

Like a jack-rabbit, Leonard swung round to go back the way he'd come – and his heart sank. There stood the daddy and the others. Leonard was trapped.

He said, 'Please!' to passers-by, but the busy world brushed him aside.

'Get off, boy!'

'Tek yourself away!' Bare-chested kids with big eyes and begging hands were nothing new in Elmina.

Leonard looked desperately from side to side. The harbour bridge was a narrow roadway with high, wrought iron sides and a hand rail – which offered him one crazy option.

He took it. With the last of his strength, his shaking feet and arms pulled him up the hand rail and on to the steel parapet above everyone's heads.

There he tottered above the derisive laughs, the blood rushing from his brain, making him dizzy.

'Come on down, Angel Boy!'

'We got work for you!'

'Come back to your daddy!'

Thirty metres below him on one side were the harbour waters, filled with hard-edged barks and canoes. Two metres below him on the other was the yelping band of street kids, three of them already running back off the bridge to get down to the water's edge.

Leonard couldn't swim. Even if he missed injury on the boats, he would drown if he jumped. His life would be over…

❀ ❀ ❀

'Leonard! Is that you, Leonard? What on earth are you doing up there?'

It was a voice from heaven.

Someone recognised him!

Leonard looked down, nearly lost his balance and only just stopped himself from falling into the water.

'Leonard, it *is* you!'

It was Chris and Vicky, the tourists he'd come with in the tro-tro to Elmina. They were squinting a bit, making sure that this bare-chested boy was the same smart kid in the scarlet school shirt that they'd treated to go into Elmina Castle with them. And the street kids were having to give ground, waiting to see what happened.

'Are you all right?' Vicky was coming nearer, climbing up a rung of the hand railings, reaching up to Leonard.

'No! I'm not!'

'Do you want help?'

'Yes! Yes, please.'

From where he was, Leonard could see the street kids coming to some sort of decision; not with words, more with pack instinct. They backed off, just a bit. To attack a tourist would not be clever.

Shaking, crying now, Leonard came warily down, helped the last metre by the strong arms of Chris from London.

'Looks like things went wrong for you,' Chris said. 'We felt rotten, losing you outside the castle. Thought you'd gone off to do your own thing…'

'Can you forgive us?' Vicky asked.

*Forgive them?* Leonard would love them for ever! But he didn't say it. He just nodded weakly; but he remembered his manners, drilled into him by Nana. 'Thank you,' he said, 'thank you',

99

as they walked off the bridge with their arms round him in the direction of Brekoso Road.

❀ ❀ ❀

It took nearly an hour and a half for Stephen Boameh to drive to Elmina. But Leonard immediately recognised the sound of those brake-discs, the clunk of the engine, the rattly slam of the driver's door when the Vauxhall pulled up. And into the office his father came, happy and angry and crying, all at the same time. He stood to attention before the sergeant as they told him how Chris and Vicky had saved his son, and he thanked them, thanked them, thanked them.

What now? All the while he had been looking at Leonard, and yet not looking at him. Now he reached across the room to grab at him, and clutched him, and gave him the biggest hug of his life; which turned into a shake, and then an arm's-length hold; and finally a straight, serious talk into Leonard's crying face, saying what a stupid thing he'd done.

And what Leonard's father said were words that the boy would never forget. 'Them quarry kids, and them abducted child soldiers in other countries, you know about them! You're a lucky, lucky boy to be coming back home!' And he wept and nodded as he spoke. 'Because... some... never do...'

And as one more hug squeezed the breath from him, Leonard pressed his face into his father's shirt, shivering with relief, and with love for this dear man. Now he realised just how precious home was, and how precious Nana was – even if she couldn't get down to low shots these days.

**BERNARD ASHLEY**'s first children's novel,
*The Trouble with Donovan Croft*, won the Other Award.
Sixteen novels have followed, establishing him as
a gritty writer in sympathy with the underdog
and winning him three shortlistings for the
Carnegie Award and the Guardian young fiction prize.
His television work has included *Running Scared*
(from which he wrote the novel), *The Country Boy*
and his adaptation of his own *Dodgem* which won
the Royal Television Society award as the best
children's entertainment of its year.
Bernard lives in South London.

**www.bashley.com**

## REBEL CARGO
### James Riordan

Abena is an Ashanti girl sold into slavery and transported on
the notorious sea-route from West Africa to Jamaica's sugar
plantations. Mungo is an English orphan who becomes a
cabin boy, only to be kidnapped and sold on as a white slave.
Mungo risks life and limb to save Abena from death, and
together they plan their escape to the Blue Mountains, to a
stronghold of runaways ruled by the legendary leader Nanny.
But can Mungo and Abena get there
before the Redcoats and their
baying bloodhounds drag them back…?

Based on events and records of the time,
the novel unflinchingly describes conditions of slavery in the
early 18th century – a time when profits took precedence
over humanity – and ends on a note of hope.

ISBN 978-1-84507-525-5

**BLACK AND WHITE**

**Rob Childs**

*Illustrated by John Williams*

Josh is soccer-mad and can't wait to show off his
ball skills to his new classmates. After all, he is the nephew
of Ossie Williams – the best footballer in the country.

Josh's arrival helps to give shy Matthew more confidence,
but it is not welcomed by Rajesh, the school goalkeeper
and captain. With important seven-a-side tournaments
coming up, will the players be able to settle her differences
and work together as a team?

ISBN978-1-84507-751-8

## BUTTER-FINGER

### Bob Cattell and John Agard

*Illustrated by Pam Smy*

Riccardo Small may not be a great cricketer –
he's only played twice before for Calypso Cricket Club –
but he's mad about the game and can tell you the
averages of every West Indies cricketer in history.
His other love is writing calypsos. Today is Riccardo's chance
to make his mark with Calypso CC against The Saints.
The game goes right down to the wire with captain
Natty and team-mates Bashy and Leo striving for victory,
but then comes the moment that changes
everything for Riccardo...

ISBN 978-1-84507-376-3

## SHINE ON, BUTTERFINGER
### Bob Cattell and John Agard
### *Illustrated by Pam Smy*

Calypso and cricket come together in the Island's Carnival,
and Riccardo has to choose between his two
passions. He has been invited to sing at the annual
Calypso Final, competing against the most famous singers
on the Island, and amidst the pan bands, the masqueraders
and the stick-fighters he discovers why the singing
competition is called 'Calypso War'. Meanwhile his
team-mates at Calypso Cricket Club are playing the most
important game in their history and their new captain,
Bashy has a lot to learn in a very short time...

ISBN 978-1-84507-626-9

## ROAR, BULL, ROAR!
### Andrew Fusek Peters and Polly Peters
*Illustrated by Anke Weckmann*

What is the real story of the ghostly Roaring Bull?
Who is the batty old lady in the tattered clothes?
Why is the new landlord such a nasty piece of work?
Czech brother and sister Jan and Marie arrive in rural
England in the middle of the night – and not everyone is
welcoming. As they try to settle into their new school,
they are plunged into a series of mysteries. Old legends
are revived as Jan and Marie unearth shady secrets in
a desperate bid to save their family from eviction.
In their quest, they find unlikely allies and deadly enemies –
who will stop at nothing to keep the past buried.

ISBN 978-1-84507-520-0

## FALCON'S FURY
### Andrew Fusek Peters and Polly Peters
*Illustrated by Naomi Tipping*

Hidden treasure … a secret crime … the precious eggs
of a bird of prey… When Jan and Marie discover who is
stealing and selling the eggs of a peregrine falcon,
they suddenly find themselves in danger. Only the ancient
legend of Stokey Castle can help them – and the falcon
will show them the way.
Andrew Fusek Peters' and Polly Peters' exciting new novel
revisits the Klecheks, a family from the Czech Republic
newly settled in Shropshire. Teenage brother and sister
Jan and Marie are soon unravelling villainy and mysteries,
but they will need even greater courage and ingenuity
to face what is about to happen.

ISBN: 978-1-84507-634-4

## CHRISTOPHE'S STORY
### Nicki Cornwell
### *Illustrated by Karin Littlewood*

Christophe has a story inside him – and this story
wants to be told. But with a new country, a new school
and a new language to cope with, Christophe can't find
the right words. He wants to tell the whole school
about why he had to leave Rwanda, why he has a bullet
wound on his chest and what happened to his baby brother,
but has he got the courage to be a storyteller?
Christophe must find a way to break through all
these barriers, so he can share his story with everyone.

ISBN 978-1-84507-521-7